The Disappearance

by

Gerry Van Hoorn

THE RED PLUME PRESS

The Red Plume Press

Petrolia, Ontario, Canada

The Disappearance

A novel by

Gerry Van Hoorn

The Disappearance

Gerry Van Hoorn

First Print Edition October 2018

Dedication

This book is dedicated to my children,

Carla and Bob Van Hoorn.

Preface

Late Saturday night, Ted went down to the casino to play the slot machines, as he did every night. He knew that he should stay away from gambling, but the temptation was too strong. This time, he would lose everything. He had borrowed money from a person with connections to the crime world. The money he borrowed, 2000 dollars, was to pay off a loan he got from his friend. He thought maybe he would have more luck this time. Ted knew what would happen when he could not come up with the money. His life would be in danger.

He needed to disappear.

Chapter 1

Ted left the casino where he had lost his money and his dignity. He knew he should have stayed away from gambling, but he was addicted to it and could not stop. He knew the consequences, and he was scared because he had borrowed money from some bad people to pay off a loan he'd gotten from his only friend. His life would be over when he could not come up with the money. What could he do other than try to disappear? But to where? He did not want to go back to his apartment where the landlord was waiting for his rent.

The only way, he thought, was to get out of the country. He had his passport in his pocket and his driver's licence. The casino was close to the border and only a short walk to the customs where truck drivers had parked their trucks. Maybe he could catch a ride with one of them? Ted took the walk to the parking lot. There were many trucks and Ted had to choose one of them. He approached a truck with a Kentucky licence and knocked on the door.

A rough looking man opened the door window and asked Ted what he wanted. Ted answered that he needed a ride to his family in the town across the border and asked the driver if he would help him. The man looked at Ted and asked him for his passport or other identification. Ted gave him his passport and the man looked at Ted again.

He said, "You can ride with me, but if they make trouble at the border, you have to go".

Ted replied, "Ok, I will take my chance".

After the trucker was ready with all the formalities to cross the border, he told Ted to get in the truck. He did not give his name and said, "Mister, you are just a passenger in my truck and you tell the customs officers the truth when they ask you something."

Ted agreed and they went on their way.

At the border checkpoint, the customs officer surprisingly did not ask any questions and the two of them went on their way across the border.

The trucker said to Ted, "Now, tell me the real reason you needed a ride. You are looking scared and running from something."

Ted answered, "I am broke and I'm running from a loan shark."

The trucker was silent and did not know what to say for a while, and then he asked, "Are you a gambler, mister?"

Ted answered, "Yes I am, and I am not proud of it."

He then told the truck driver that he could let him go anytime he wanted to get rid of him, and that he was very thankful for his help.

The trucker shook his head and said, "You people never learn to get rid of bad habits. You can ride with me until the night and then you will have to find your own way. I hope that the Lord will be with you on your further travels where ever you may go. I cannot support you."

Ted was surprised at the man's answer. He thought that the man was a rough truck driver. Ted remained quiet for a while. Minutes later, he asked the trucker for his name and also asked if he was a Christian. The trucker replied, "Yes I am, and my name is Paul West and now you think I am a lunatic, right?"

Ted answered quickly, "No, no, I think you are a great man but I am surprised because I did not expect this. My apologies."

After a while, Ted asked Paul if he was married and whether he had any children. Paul told Ted that he was married and that he had 3 children, two girls and a boy, whom he loved very much. He wished he could stay at home to enjoy his family but truck driving was all he knew, and he needed the money to supports his family. He could not understand why some people would gamble their hard-earned money away and he had no respect for them that did.

Ted sat silently for a while and then he told Paul, not to give him an excuse, his story of why he became a gambler. He had had a good job and was happy with his life. His dad was an army soldier who had died on an assignment overseas. Ted then was living with his mother until he graduated from college. She became ill and she then died after a short fight with her illness. Ted, in his grief, could not get over losing his mother and started gambling.

Now he was in trouble and did not know what to do with his life.

Paul had respect for Ted's honest and dreadful story but he told Ted that there would have been many other ways to get over his sorrow. For instance, when he had more faith in himself and was not a weakling, he would get over his sorrow. Or if he had trusted in the Lord Almighty, he would have survived his ordeal. But it was not up to him to judge Ted.

For an hour both men rode along in silence, but something was going through the mind of Ted. What would be his future, who would help him next? He was interrupted in his thought by a sudden stop of the truck. They were in a city parking lot and Paul said, "Well Ted, here ends your ride and I hope you will find your way through the rest of your life. May God bless you."

Ted asked Paul not to tell anybody that he had been with him, for his life's sake. Paul said, "I will tell the truth but only should they ask me. As for the rest, it will be as if I have never seen you before."

Ted told Paul that he was very thankful for the ride and for his encouragement, and he climbed down from the truck and walked away across the parking lot.

Chapter 2

Ted looked around, not knowing what to do next. He was still thinking about the things that Paul had told him but he knew that it was too late for him to go back. He needed a place to sleep but he had no money. The only place to sleep would be a bench in the park or under a bridge. Ted started walking through the city and then he saw a sign for the Salvation Army. He had heard so much about this organization and thought that he should check it out for a place to sleep.

He knocked at the door and a lady in uniform opened the door and asked him if he needed help. Boy, do I ever, Ted thought. Ted told her that he had no money and he needed a place to sleep. The lady told him that if he was not using drugs or alcohol, he was welcome. Ted felt so bad but he told the lady that he was not a drug or alcohol addict.

The lady looked him over and said, "You come in and I will find you a place to sleep." When he stepped inside, he could smell the food in the kitchen and he realised that he had not eaten since the night before. The lady saw the look on his face and told him that he could have dinner, too.

Ted ate his meal with a few homeless people. He was given a cot to sleep on in the same room where these homeless people were also sleeping.

It was for Ted, a sleepless night. He was thinking about what Paul had told him and listening to the snoring of the other people in the room. Inside, he was still rebellious and did not want to give up his old way of living.

The next day he was given a modest breakfast and after that, another Salvation Army person wanted to talk to him. She asked him where he came from, what had happened to him and why he hadn't any money. He told her that he could not give her his name as he was a fugitive and in danger if she were to give his name to other people. Ted explained that he was addicted to gambling but that he wanted to change his life. He also told her what the truck driver had told him.

She was understanding and promised that she would not ask any more questions. As he went to leave, she wished him the blessings of the Lord and that she hoped he would find his way, and that he was welcome to come back again when he was in dire need.

When Ted was outside he began thinking about how to find his way. Where could he go from here?

A voice behind him startled him out of his thoughts. He turned around to see a man asking him for money. Ted had only 50 cents in his pocket and he gave it to man. The man looked at the money and said, "Is that all you have?" Ted just turned around and walked away to the next street, off to the unknown.

A few blocks further down the street there were stores and some restaurants. In the window of one of the restaurants there was a sign that said, "Dishwasher wanted". Ted knew he had to eat and he had no money so he did not hesitate and was inside the restaurant before he realised what he was doing.

A waitress came to him and thought he was a customer and asked him if he wanted to sit in a booth or at a table. Ted said that he was there to inquire about the dishwasher's job. The waitress called the manager over, and a lady came and spoke to Ted about the job. She wondered why a man like Ted would need such a job, but it was only for two weeks and she needed the help. She told him that he could start right away if possible.

Ted said he was able to start immediately so the lady took him to the kitchen and gave him some instructions. Before he knew it, he was working, cleaning pots and pans. The plates, cups and silverware were going into a dishwashing machine.

Now he had a job and the table leftovers for food but where could he find a place to sleep? Could he go back to the Salvation Army station? The waitress came into the kitchen and asked for his name. He did not know what to say and thought for a moment and told her his name was Alex (he did not lie, really, because his second name was Alexander).

The waitress said that her name was Mary and she told him that the busiest time of the restaurant was at night, but that she only worked in the mornings. He could see in her eyes that she was thinking the same thought as the manager.

It was indeed a very busy night in the restaurant, and Ted had to work hard to keep up with the waitresses. He could feel that this was unusual work for him and one of the waitresses asked what kind of work he did before, but he gave no answer. When the restaurant was closing, he had an idea. He asked the manager if he could stay overnight in the restaurant and sleep on the floor.

The lady looked at him. She was surprised at his question and she did not like what he was asking. She asked Ted why he needed to sleep on the floor here. Did he have no other place to sleep?

To his own surprise, he spun a tale about how his wife had kicked him to the street and that he had no place to sleep (although in truth, he had kicked himself to the street). The lady told him that it was against the rules to sleep in the restaurant but he could stay in a room in her apartment building for one night. After that, he would have to find another place. He drove with the manager lady to the apartment building and he was given a visitors' room for the night. The next morning, she would pick him up to go to work.

Chapter 3

Ted was getting used to the dishwasher's job and he got to know the waitresses. Some of them were asking questions about his life but he gave them only what they wanted to hear. He made arrangements with the lady at the Salvation Army to sleep there for the time being. He promised that it would be no longer than 2 weeks. Ted met a homeless man, who was also sleeping at the Salvation Army building, who told him that, sometimes people traveled free but illegally, in railroad boxcars. Ted had asked the man where the railroad station was and the man gave him directions. It was not that far from the restaurant.

Before his second work week was over, he asked the manager to give him his last payment in cash money and she did not mind because she suspected that he had no credit card or bank account. When he left the restaurant, he thanked the manager for the job she had given to him. It was already late in the night. He had said goodbye to the lady of the Salvation Army. Ted made his way to the railroad station. He had to be smart to find out where the railroad cars were going. He certainly did not want to go back to Buffalo and Canada where he came from.

When he entered the railroad yard, there were a few men checking the box cars. Ted stayed out of sight and had to wait until they passed before he could enter the yard. When he walked along the track, he saw that some of the cars had a destination on the side. They all were going to New York City but there were some empty box cars in the train chain. Ted chose one of the empty box cars and before he opened the side door, he looked around to make sure nobody was in the yard. Before he knew it, he was inside the box car. It was dark inside and he went looked around for a good place to sit himself down.

While he was making himself comfortable, he heard some noise. He took out his cigarette lighter, switched it on and he saw that he was not alone. In the opposite corner were a woman and a child. He looked at them with disbelief. He asked the woman why they were there.

The woman told him that she had to go New York City but had no money. She said that one of her friends from the railroad yard had put her in this boxcar. Ted asked her if she would mind if he was in the same car, too. She hesitated for a moment, not knowing what to say, but when Ted explained his situation, she said that she did not mind.

He asked the woman if she had eaten and if the child needed something. She said that she and her child had no food or drink since the day before. He opened his backpack and took out some sandwiches that he was given from the restaurant, and offered them to the woman, who took them gratefully. Ted went back to his corner and took out a blanket to sit on and ate his sandwich.

The night was getting cooler and he was lucky to have his jacket on. He was wondering about the woman and her child. Did she have no husband or family? He took his blanket and gave it to the woman and her child to stay warm. He sat on his backpack and closed his jacket. They all settled down to try to get a bit of sleep.

Early in the morning, the train started moving with a slow speed and lots of noise. It was not so comfortable sitting on the floor of the car. Some light of the morning sun peeked into the car and Ted looked at the woman and her child. They were sitting close to each other and he noticed that the child was a girl. When they awoke, he gave them his last sandwich and a sip out of his water bottle. The train was speeding up and the whistle blew as it passed every main road or city.

Later, the woman told him that they would be in New York City by nightfall. She was thankful for the food he had given to her. She was going to friends in New York because she wanted to get away from the place they were living. Ted did not ask questions as he did not want to know what was going in their lives. He told her to say that, when asked, that she had never seen him before. He wished that he hadn't met her but hoped that he would be safe.

Chapter 4

When they arrived in New York City, they had to sneak off the train and out of the train yard without being seen by other people. Ted opened the door, looked out of the boxcar and noticed that at that side, there were no other trains. It wouldn't be a good idea to go out of that side because there were no trains to hide behind. When he opened the door at the other side, he saw that another train was beside them. He told the woman that it was best to leave the box car on this side. He helped the woman down and then carried the girl out of the boxcar. They walked carefully between the trains to the light. They assumed that the light was where there must be the entrance into the railyard. Also, the front of the train was there at the lights. It was a 500-foot walk through the area.

When they came close to the lights, they saw a small office building. They had to cross the yard to get to the entrance and out of the yard. Ted had to think of something to divert the attention of the men in the office without getting into trouble. He got a crazy idea and he told the woman.

Ted would go to the office and tell them that his daughter was missing and that the woman would appear with the girl in the open. She agreed. Ted went to the office to talk to the men there, and he was surprised that they had not noticed him, but it was too late for a change. He told the man about the 'lost' girl and then woman showed up as planned. The men did not seem to care about it and did not ask any questions and let them leave the yard.

When they were out of the yard, walking to the next street, Ted asked the woman what she was planning to do. She told him that she was going to look for a telephone booth to call her friends to pick her up. After they found a telephone, she called her friends and they were coming to pick them up. Ted waited with her until her friends arrived and then he left in the direction of nowhere. He had no idea where to go. He just kept on walking until he found a small park with a bench where he took a rest. He was amazed with his luck so far. It seemed all so easy.

Chapter 5

He must have fallen asleep on the bench. When he awoke, it was to the noise of a dog. The dog sniffed him and his owner came to see what he was doing. It was a woman and she wished him good morning. Before she went on her way, he asked her for the directions to the New York City harbour. She didn't know exactly where that was but she knew that it was not close by. The woman said that there was a library in the next street and he could find out via street maps there, the direction to the harbour. He was happy with her advice.

It was still early so he relaxed on the bench until nine o'clock and then he went to look for the library. It was in a large building on the second street. It was already open when he got there so he went inside. He did not know where to look for a map. A young man asked him if he could help him. He said that he needed a city map for directions to the nearby harbour. The young man was very helpful and made him a map that he could take with him for directions. Ted was very happy and said thanks to the young man.

When he looked on the map as the young man was making it for him, he saw that it was quite a distance to walk so he asked the man if there was a city bus or street car going that way and he was helped with that too. Now he hoped that he had enough money to be able to take the bus.

Ted was hungry but did not want to eat just yet. He found the bus stop a couple of streets farther out. When the bus came, he asked the driver how much the fare was to the harbour. The bus driver told him that he was not going that far, but that the end of his run was not that far from the harbour. He gave the amount of the fare, which was an amount Ted could afford to pay. When Ted was settled in the bus, the driver asked him if he was a sailor and Ted told him he was not, but that he was looking for a job in the harbour.

The bus trip took almost an hour and Ted noticed that he was coming into a poor neighbourhood within an industrial area. When he left the bus, the driver told him good luck with finding a job. He gave Ted some directions to the harbour.

By now, Ted was hungry and he had only a few dollars to spend. He saw a small coffee shop where he bought a cup of coffee, which was all he could afford. In the shop were a few young men looking at him but they did not ask him any questions. Ted did not think about it. He left the shop on his way to the harbour in the direction the bus driver had given to him.

A few blocks away, Ted heard some noise behind him. When he turned to see who was there, he saw the two men from the coffee shop. They told him that they wanted his money and when he told them that he had no money, they attacked him violently. Ted tried to get away from them but it did not help. He defended himself as far he could and gave a few good defensive hits. To his surprise, another man came to his aid. This man told the young men to get lost or they would be arrested. As they ran away, he told Ted to get out of the area as soon as possible, because they would be coming back for him. The man must have been an undercover policeman, Ted thought.

Happy to get away with only a few scratches, he walked as fast as possible to get away from the neighbourhood. He started thinking about the tragic situation of his gambling and the state he was in. No home, no work, no money and nothing to eat.

Strange enough, he was not hungry and he was wondering how long he could be without any food or water. He pushed the thought away and kept walking as fast as possible.

After two hours of walking and getting closer to the harbour, he could hear the sound of ships. It was getting busy with trucks and cars coming and going to the harbour. Here, he would hopefully find a job and start a new life.

Chapter 6

In the town where Ted used to live, there was a search going on for him. It was already three weeks after his disappearance. No family members were missing him because they did not care too much. The landlord of the apartment building where Ted had lived went to the police to get permission to enter his apartment. They did not find anything that would show where he could be and the police advised the landlord to go to a lawyer to get an eviction for his tenant. Until then, he could not do anything. The police, however, made a missing person report, which would be run in the newspaper after another week.

Bolstero, the man who had loaned the money to Ted, went on a search for Ted along with his buddies. They went to the casino to ask if they could take a look at the footage from the surveillance cameras, but the manager of the casino told them to go first to the police. They came back later with the police who were also looking for Ted because he was now a missing person.

The cameras from the casino, outside and inside the building, did not reveal anything other than Ted leaving the casino and walking away down the street. Bolstero did not give up so easy because he had the loaned 2000 dollars at stake. He kept on searching and asking questions all over town. He had some connections with people who were living across the border and he tried to get some information from customs but to no avail.

The landlord eventually got permission to empty Ted's apartment and to store whatever was of value for one year and after he could dispose of the items as he pleased.

Chapter 7

The harbour was an enormous complex with many entrances. Along the harbour were many streets and buildings. Ted had to find a way to get something to eat and drink. He saw a person who looked like somebody who was working in the area, so he stopped the man with the question, "Sir, I am looking for work in the harbour or on a ship. Can you please tell me where to go?"

The man looked at him and said, "There is an office farther up on this street, and in the window, they have a sign that says 'Help wanted'. Maybe you can ask them? Maybe not what you are looking for, but you never know."

He went on to say, "By the looks of it, I think you need something to eat. There is a sailors' home nearby where you possibly can get something to drink and to eat."

Ted said thanks to the man and went in to the direction of the office. It was very busy on the street and by now, it was getting late in the afternoon. When he arrived in the office, he was just in time because in an hour, they were going to close. He asked what kind of help they wanted and they were surprised. They were not expected to see someone his age. Ted told them that he needed a job because he needed to eat.

They told him if he had a driver's licence and a good record he could work for them until the end of the month.

It was only temporary work and that was fine with Ted. They said he could start the next day. When everything was settled, he left for the sailors' home.

The sailors' home was similar to the Salvation Army kind of operation. Ted was welcomed and they gave him something to eat and to drink. When he asked the lady of the sailors' home if he could stay overnight, she said that it was not possible but she told him to go to the next street where there was a Salvation Army building. Ted thanked the people of the home and went on his way.

He found shelter for the night in the Salvation Army home where he would stay for a couple of nights.

Chapter 8

Ted left the Salvation Army building the next morning to start his new-found work. His job as a delivery person started with a ride to the harbour's office. He had an identification card to get through the gate and when he came to the office to drop off his mail, he met a very nice person who would later help him with a job on a ship.

Ted was tired and hungry when he finished his day of work. He went to the soup kitchen to see if he could get some food. When he entered the building where they serve the people, he saw that he was not the only person. There was a lineup and Ted felt embarrassed to be there, but the hunger took away his pride. When it was his turn, he looked at the lady behind the table and he recognised her. She was the lady he met in the harbour office. She gave him a bowl of soup and a dinner plate. When he was sitting to eat his meal, the lady came over to his table and asked if she could ask him some questions. Ted noticed that she was a soft-spoken woman. He said that she could ask him any question. The first question surprised him; she asked him if he was married and the second question was if he had a place to sleep.

Ted's answer was "No lady, I am not married and I am going to the Salvation Army for the night."

She was quiet for a moment, then she asked, "Are you in some kind of trouble or running away from something?"

He said that he did not want to talk about it.

The lady introduced herself and said that her name is Betsie and asked him to come back the next day she would like to talk to him.

When she left, he was ready to go. When he was on his way to the Salvation Army station, he was thinking of the woman and her soft-spoken voice. She was a few years younger than Ted and not bad looking. Was he falling in love? No, he did not want to think about that.

That night he was so tired that he did not undress before sleeping on his cot. Luck seemed to be with him, because one of the people in the room had robbed some other person. Everybody had to disclose their possessions and Ted was cleared and allowed to leave.

When he came to his work he had not eaten but he was not hungry. He had a full day of work and it was late when he came back to the office. The office was closed and he parked the van in the parking place behind the office. He was too late for the soup kitchen so he decided to sleep in the van. He did not want to go to the Salvation Army again. Ted thought about his miserable situation and about the lady from the soup kitchen. He promised himself that he would go the next day to see the lady from the soup kitchen. The sleeping in the van was not that great but he managed to get a little rest.

When he left his work the next day to go to the soup kitchen for something to eat, Betsie was not there. After his dinner, he went to the Salvation Army building to see if he could stay overnight.

The next day was not that busy and Ted managed to clean himself up a little in the washroom of the office before he went to work. He had to make a delivery to the harbour office again. When he came in the office, the same lady (Betsie) who helped him before was there. She told him that she worked as a volunteer in the soup kitchen. She asked why he was not there last night and he told her that he was too late for the soup kitchen but that he would be there tonight. He told her that he would be happy to have something to eat.

Chapter 9

A big change was coming in Ted's life

It was already Friday when he had finished his work and Ted had his first pay. He told his employer that he preferred cash money and of course, it was only temporarily work they had agreed upon. He went straight to the soup kitchen because by now he was very hungry. Betsie was there and she gave him an extra portion of meat and potatoes. She asked him to wait after supper for her. When she was finished they could go somewhere to talk.

Ted enjoyed his dinner and the cup of coffee. He had never been so hungry in his life. After he finished, he asked for another cup of coffee and waited outside the building for Betsie. When she came outside, they decided to go to a coffee shop to talk. He felt that he could trust her, and he told her what had happened to him. She remained quiet and listened to him with patience.

Betsie asked Ted if he knew that he could be in trouble if he was stopped by the police and they found out that he had no green card to work in the US. He told her that he knew about all of this, and the only thing he wanted to do was to get on board of a ship to get as far as possible away from the men who were looking for him. Betsie understood his situation and felt sorry for him. She had an idea and asked him if he had a place to sleep. He told her about the Salvation Army and she told him to go with her to her home instead. She had a spare bedroom for him to use and that he could use her facilities to clean himself up. He could stay with her until he had a green card. Betsie had some connections to be able to help him as long as he took care of himself. He asked Betsie why she w willing to help him. She hardly knew him and he did not want to take advantage of her goodness, but Betsie answered, "I believe in the Lord Jesus Christ and I, am here to help people as best I can and I think I can trust you." Again, Ted was surprised about the people he met whom had so much faith.

He could not believe his luck when they went to Betsie's place. She lived in a small house in a quiet working-class neighbourhood, on a street with lots of trees. Her home was cozy and with modest furniture and very clean. Betsie told him where his room was and showed the bathroom facility he could use. There were towels and other toiletries for him to use. She told him to clean up because she could see that he had not taken care of himself. There were also clothes in the bedroom drawers and he could use whatever he needed for the time being. Ted looked in the bedroom with a real bed, the kind he had not slept in for weeks. He told Betsie that he was very thankful for her help and that he would not disappoint her.

Before he went to take a bath, they talked some more about their lives. Betsie was a widow and she had no children. She was 2 years younger than Ted.

Ted told Betsie that he was never married and as soon as he had a job as a sailor, he would pay her back for everything she had done for him. She told Tev that for now he did not have to worry but to just get a good night sleep. On Monday she would drop him off at his work. Betsie said goodnight and went to her own room and closed her door with a lock.

Ted slept through the whole night and he woke up by the noise he heard in the kitchen. He looked around in his room and saw the things he did not see the night before. There were a few pictures on the wall of Betsie and her previous husband and some of other people, maybe her parents? On the night table there lay a bible. He had not noticed this when he went to sleep. He was still not used to a religion, and never bothered to think about it. He put the thought of all this out of his mind and got out of bed to go to the washroom to wash up and get dressed.

When he came into the kitchen, he smelled the fresh coffee. Betsie was in her morning coat and they said good morning to each other at the same time. They laughed.

Betsie made breakfast for the both of them. Ted felt good and still could not believe that what had happened to him wasn't just a dream. He looked over at Betsie while she was eating and he noticed that she had a young and pretty face. Ted asked her what she is going to do for the rest of the day and also asked what he could do for her. Betsie said that she had to do some shopping and that he could stay at home if he had no other plans.

He felt that she trusted him and he did not understand why she took the risk with a stranger like himself. He did not want to ask her about it, but he said to her, "Betsie, you don't know me but you'll let me stay in your house while you go shopping?"

She looked at him with a smile and said, "Sometimes, you have to take a risk and hope for the best!"

She told him that she liked him as a friend and that he resembled her husband. She did not mind having a man in her house for a while.

That day after the shopping was done, they played some games and then watched TV until bedtime. He went to his room and he took the bible from the night table. He opened it up to the page where there was a book marker. He read a little but he did not understand much of it, so he put the book away and went to sleep.

The next day he woke up early and after he was dressed, he went to the kitchen and to his surprise, Betsie was already dressed to go out. She told Ted that she was going to church and if he felt like it, he could go with her. He told her that he had never been to church and that he didn't think he was ready for it yet but, if she really wanted him to go with her, he would do so. She understood his thoughts and said that she was going by herself and would be going to visit some friends after church. He could stay at home and would have to take care of himself for lunch.

Later that day, they had dinner together and they talked about some common interests. They enjoyed themselves and evening went by fast. Tomorrow they had to go to work.

After a good night's sleep and a real tasty breakfast, Betsie drove Ted to work with the promise that she would pick him up after work.

Chapter 10

Ted continued to live in Betsie's home, and he was getting used to his new life. Betsie delivered on her promise to help him get a green card so that he did not have to worry about his job. Ted had an interview with a merchant shipping company for a job as a sailor. If he was accepted, he would be away for a long time. He really did not mind. The next week, he was asked to come to the office to give some more information and to answer a few health questions. After all the formalities, Ted was accepted for the sailor's position and was told to report to the ship the next Monday.

Betsie was happy for Ted having found new work but she was also sad that he was leaving her. She did not let him know how much she would miss him. She gave him some of her husband's clothes and made sure that he had everything he would need for the time he would be away. Later, before he was due to leave, she secretly put some extra things in his bag.

She didn't know when Ted was coming back to her and she asked him to let her know, once in a while, how he was doing.

Meanwhile, Ted's delivery job was finished and he received his last pay. He told the people in the office that he was very thankful for the opportunity they had given to him to work for them and for all the help and trust they'd given him. When departed from the office, he left his identification card and harbour permit behind. He decided to give his last payment to Betsie, to cover a little of the cost of all she had done for him.

When Betsie picked him up from the office, they decided to go to a restaurant for dinner. When they had finished their meal, Ted paid for the dinner and he tried to give her his money, but she refused to accept it. He told her that he would be honoured if she would allow him to pay her back a little bit for all her hospitality, and with that, she accepted the money.

The weekend would be the last of their time together before Ted left on the ship, and Betsie did her best to make it as cozy as possible. She tried not to show her feelings but it was very difficult. This was true for Ted as well. He was well aware that his feelings were more than just friends where Betsie was concerned, but he knew that he did not deserve her love.

On Monday, Betsie drove Ted to the harbour where his ship was docked. They did not speak during the ride and both were kind of sad that they had to say good bye to each other and might never see each other again. When they arrived, Ted got out the car with his backpack. He hesitated for a moment, then he looked at Betsie, took her in his arms and gave her a big kiss. He said with tears in his eyes, "Betsie, you are the best and most beautiful woman a man could wish to have in his life. God bless you."

Betsie gave him a kiss and hurried to get back in the car so Ted could not see her tears. She left, waving to him. Ted was on his own, going to a new adventure.

Chapter 11

Ted found the ship he was going to sail on. It looked old and unimpressive to him as he walked along the dock, but when he came aboard the ship, things did not seem so bad. Someone on the deck gave him the directions to the cabin of the captain of the ship.

When Ted introduced himself, the captain welcomed him to the ship and told him what his duties were and made him aware of the regulations for the crew. Ted found out he would be sharing a cabin with three other sailors. The next day, they would leave the harbour with the destination of Hamburg, Germany.

Ted went to the cabin where he met two other sailors, both were young men. Ted told them that his name was Alex (his middle name) and that he had never sailed before. They told him that whenever you sail out of a harbour, it is always like a first time. They had sailed before but they were new to this ship, like Ted. A fourth sailor was still to come, as well as a boatsman.

When he was settled, with his private things stored in his locker and his bed made, he found a note from Betsie along with a small bible. She wrote that she wished him a safe journey and that she would pray that he would come back to her someday because she loved him. She also told him that in a time of loneliness, he would find peace by reading his little bible. She also asked him to please write and let her know where he would be in the coming times. Ted felt sorry that he left her but he could not go back.

Back in his home town, things were going in another direction. The man Bolstero, who had been searching for Ted was in a fatal car accident. The police and other people were no longer looking for Ted anymore. He was not an important case and not a criminal according to the police, so if Ted had known all about this, his life maybe would have gone in a different direction.

The ship left the harbour and Ted started working with the other sailors to winch in the ropes, store equipment and then they started to paint part of the ship. The weather was reasonably good. When they were out of the harbour, Ted felt some seasickness coming on. He did not give in to it and kept on working as best as he could. Later that day, the ship's bell rang and it was time for lunch. After a few sandwiches, Ted felt a lot better but still, he was not used to being a sailor. He worked the whole day, doing all kinds of tasks but mostly painting. He got along well with the boatsman, who was a few years older than him.

The day went fast and he liked the fresh air at sea. The other sailors were easy to get along with. They had their own mess hall and the cook brought them food. He was hungry and tired when he started his dinner. To his surprise, the boatman asked if anyone would like to pray before eating but nobody did. It made Ted think of Betsie and wonder what she was doing at this time. If he had been in a different situation, he would have asked her to marry him. But he was just a loser in his mind. The other sailors brought him out of his thoughts and asked him where he was from. He did not want to tell them that he was from Canada so he told them that he was from New York and that he was a single person who lost his job. He did not lie about this.

They talked about some general things and they seemed to get along with each other. Later in the cabin, they shared some common interests and before he knew it, Ted was in his bed for a good night sleep.

Meanwhile, Betsie had trouble forgetting the man who was in her life for a short time. She had not realized that she loved him so much. He was a sincere person who did not take advantage of her in the time they were living in the same house. Every night, Betsy prayed for him and asked the Lord to take care of him and when possible, to bring him back to her. She knew that her prayers were not always answered but she would not give up. She found rest and hope in her work, and in her volunteering work in the soup kitchen.

Chapter 12

When they were two days into their voyage to Hamburg, the ship came into some difficulty. One of the engines running the propellers of the ship had to be shut down for repairs, which did slow down the speed of the ship. The weather was not good which made sailing more uncomfortable for the crew.

Luckily, the chief engineer was capable to fix the problem in a short amount of time. The ship however, was off course and it would be a longer sail to Hamburg. Ted did not know how much work there was to do on board of a ship. The cargo on board of the ship consisted of large containers with automobiles from an American motor company. Every day, they had to inspect the cargo space to make sure everything was kept in its place, especially during some rough weather. When they were close to the English Channel, the sea was rough with stormy weather. The crew, by now, were used to that kind of weather and also Ted was no longer prone to much seasickness.

When they arrived in Hamburg, they had to unload the cargo. A hoist and crane had to be installed and that was a big job for the sailors. Carefully, the containers with the automobiles were taken out of the cargo space and Ted learned in a short time how to maneuver the hoist. It took two days to fully unload the cargo space and onto the waiting trucks. The crew was happy that everything went smoothly and they were ready for their supper. That night they all were quite tired. There was no time for conversation because they all went to bed.

Ted was anxious to know where the ship would go next. He had sent Betsie a letter to let her know that he was thinking of her and what he was doing while on the ship. He wrote that he would like to come back to her as soon as his ship sailed back to New York, and that he would never leave her anymore.

He did not know what would happen to him later on.

The crew had one day to go ashore to do shopping or whatever they wanted to do. Ted preferred to stay on the ship. He did not want to spend any money. Later that day, the boatsman informed them that the next port of call of the ship would be Oslo, Norway. They would pick up a load of windmill materials and generators for the next stop.

Late in the day, the ship was ready to sail and they set off to sea again. The weather was not that good and with no ballasts, it was a risky sail thru the waters between Germany and Norway, well-known for being dangerous.

The sail was as bad as it could be. The ship, without ballast, was as a toy in the water but the captain had lots of experience, and the crew hoped for the best. There was not much to do on the deck for the sailors and they had to stay below deck anyway.

It was a long night for Ted because he was not feeling well and to lie in bed was not helping his seasickness. The ship was bouncing around on the waves. He thought of being a sailor his whole life was not for him.

The next morning, they had to get to work on the deck. The weather was a lot better and they were getting close to the Oslo harbour. The view of the Norway coastline was so beautiful with all the mountains. This is one of the good things about being a sailor, Ted thought.

When the ship was docked in the harbour, they had no time to relax because right away, they had to unload the cargo. Everything was stored in large crates and it was very difficult to maneuver to get the load into the cargo space. Ted and one of the other sailors were operating the large beam from the crane when something went wrong. The beam turned the wrong way and it swept Ted off the deck and into the water. He was kind of dizzy and he was not a good swimmer so he almost drowned before they could get him out of the water. He was not able to work right away but luckily, he had no injury other than a headache and a shock of his life. He thought that night about what would happen if he got swept off the deck out at sea? He did not want to think about it. Before he went to sleep, he took some of the pain medication that Betsie had put in his pack.

The next day they would sail to The Netherlands with the destination of the port of Rotterdam.

Ted was dreaming that night and one of the other sailors had to wake him up because he had a nightmare. He had a good relationship with the other sailors, Bart, Sean and Robert. They knew that he was not a real sailor in his heart but they enjoyed his happy outlook on life. They knew that he would never sail after they went back home. The ship had a pleasant crew and what was also very important; they had a good cook to keep everyone happy.

Two days later, they arrived in the port of Rotterdam, a large harbour. They had a pilot on board to maneuver them to the dock site. For economical reasons, they could not stay long in the port. That night was the only time they had to go on shore if they wanted. The dock site was close to the centre of the city and Ted decided to go for a walk to stretch his legs and do some sightseeing. Walking down one of the streets of the city, he saw that it was very busy with people shopping. He was taking in the sights when he passed an alley where he was attacked by two young men. They wanted his money and when he told them that he had no money, they began to beat him. People around him were not doing anything to help him. Again, luck was with him. A police officer came to his aid and brought him back to his ship.

He said thanks to the police officer and he went back on board the ship. He had some injuries but nothing serious. With some bandages, he could manage. The other sailors were asking him what happened, and when he told them, they said to him, "Man you are lucky to be back and not dead in some alley of the city."

Ted went to his locker and took the little bible Betsie gave to him he started reading some of the pages and on one of them, it said, "But search first for the Kingdom of the Lord and his righteousness, and all these things will be added to you." Ted went to a quiet place on the deck of the ship and bowed his head and for the first time, he prayed to the Lord. He asked for forgiveness and thanked the Lord for saving him through all his troubles and asked that he might be able to go back to Betsie.

After his praying he felt a lot different. as if a burden fell of his shoulders and he felt peace in his heart. He went back to the cabin to sleep. The next morning would be very busy for the crew.

Chapter 13

The very efficient unloading in Rotterdam harbour made it a lot easier for Ted and the other sailors because they only had to supervise to see that everything went smoothly and without damaging the cargo. Ted noticed that there was a lot of security around the dock site. He did not notice this in the other harbours they'd been in. When the unloading was done, the customs officers came on board, which happened in every harbour, to check the ship for illegal drugs and the like. In the sailors' quarters was nothing to offend but still they checked the lockers and everything in the cabin. It took a while before the ship was allowed to leave.

The ship was leaving the harbour right after they had taken in fuel for the engines. There was no new cargo to be loaded and their new destination was Liverpool, England. Again, the ship had no ballast and the sea in the canal was very rough. Once again, this would be again a miserable sail over to Liverpool, the city of "The Beatles".

When they were halfway to Liverpool, an alarm went off on the ship. There was a fire on board and everyone was ordered to the deck. Luckily, it was only a small fire in the cook's galley. It was extinguished by the cook himself. For the rest of the sail they were busy cleaning up the galley and everything had to be painted again. No food was spoiled and that was a miracle!

At the harbour in Liverpool, they would be loading the ship with domestic water. Arriving in the harbour, the boatsman told one of the sailors that after they had taken on the new cargo, he would like to go to a soccer game that night and he wanted somebody to go with him. That was a great idea and they all said that they would go with him as long they could get some tickets. The first mate, Art Bos, had some information taken via the radio and he had spoken with a person from the seamen's home in the city. They would get tickets for them to go to see the soccer game.

The new cargo was English-built automobiles. It took the whole day to load and stow the new cargo in place and secure it for the sail to New York. That night, a van from the seamen's home arrived to take them to the soccer stadium. They had very good seats and they enjoyed the view. Ted had never been in a stadium before because he was not a sports fan. He could not believe his eyes and ears because before the game start there is always a kind of sing-along. In the middle of the field there was a band playing typical English songs and everybody was singing along with the music. A man was directing the crowd and sang along with the public so everybody knew the lyrics.

The game started right on time. Liverpool was playing against Chelsea. The game was very tight and the sailors enjoyed themselves. It was well worth the money to have an experience like this away from the ship. The boatsman was absorbed in the game and when they drove back to the ship, he was full of joy, talking about the game. It was good to be together as colleges and as friends. After the game, they all went back to the ship. It was already late so they all went to bed because tomorrow, they had to work.

Chapter 14

Finally, the ship's next destination would be New York. Ted was fired up and he hoped that nothing would happen on this last trip and that they would arrive safe. He was looking forward to see Betsie again. He was also thinking about what he should do for work when he got back. Certainly, there would be no more sailing for him.

It was a long day before they were ready to sail from the Liverpool harbour into the sea. That night, Ted walked over the deck to his favorite place on the ship where he enjoyed the evening, reading his little bible book. When he went to sit down, one of the sailors (Bart) came and sat beside him. He asked Ted if he was religious. Ted answered that he was not but he wanted to know all about it. To his surprise, Bart told him that he could help him if he had some questions. The two men begun the kind of conversation that Ted never would have expected from this young sailor. He learned a lot from Bart and he started to understand some of the things he read. Bart told him also that, beside the cook and Ted, they were all married. Ted told him about Betsie and that he would like to take a job on shore to stay close to her. Bart said he understood, the life of a sailor away from his family is hard, but that they would miss him after he left the ship. Later, when Bart left him alone, Ted started to think about his life.

He grew up as an only child in a family. His dad was an army soldier and his mother worked as a nurse. As far as he knew, his family did not practice a religion and did not go to a church. His dad died on an assignment overseas and Ted grew up with just his mother. He finished high school and after he graduated, he took a course in mechanical engineering at the local college.

His mother, however, became ill, and she could not work anymore. Beside his studies, Ted worked part-time in different places. She died after shortly after Ted graduated from college. Ted received a small survivor benefit from the army, which he used to pay for a storage unit. He wanted to save some of the valuable things of his Mom and Dad. All the funeral arrangements for his mother were already arranged by her and by the funeral home.

They had a small family gravesite and Ted would go there every month for a visit and would leave some flowers. He had a hard time getting used to being without his mother. She had been a very big part in his life and he could not get over his loss.

Ted had made arrangement with the bank for the monthly payments for the storage unit. Later, he would have to decide what to do with it. He left the apartment he had shared with his mother and rented a cheaper place to live. Back when he was in high school Ted had had a girlfriend which he really liked, but her family moved away to another province and he lost track of her. He tried so hard to locate her or to phone her but he had no success in ever finding her. She disappeared and never contacted him. Ted then got a job as draftsman in an office. He did not have very many friends. He was getting used to living alone without any other family around. He didn't have much contact with his neighbours. Not so much later, he became addicted to gambling, and that is where this story started. Ted thought about what would have happened to him if he had not had so much luck.

All the people he met on his journey were very good to him, like Paul, the truck driver. Another fact was that they all were religious. Was there any meaning to all of this, or was it all a coincidence? His shipmate, Bart, was just a stranger and he had no reason to help explain what Ted was reading. The Salvation Army and the soup kitchen with the lovely lady Betsie was that all a coincidence, or were they all tokens to direct his life?

When Ted thought of Betsie, he felt that he became another person. He hoped that he could make her happy. Only a few more days of sailing and they would be together. Finding a steady job was Ted's first priority.

Chapter 15

Betsie received the letter from Ted. She had been wondering if he would ever come back to her. So many things could happen with a ship out at sea. And sometimes, people would change after a long time separated from each other but she did not want to think about all of this.

The next day, she phoned the shipping company to get some information about the destinations of the ship. She asked the person whom she spoke with, a person she knew from the church, to please keep her informed about the ship and the crew. It was so quiet in her home and Betsie had never noticed this before. She thought about why she noticed the quiet now. Was it the man who came into her life that made this change? Was it because she was busy with volunteering for the soup kitchen and with her work during the day that she had no time to think about all of this? No, she was sure it was because of the man who took her heart and left. Normally Betsie always slept well, but lately she spent her nights thinking of Ted and where he could be at that moment.

That Monday, 5 weeks after Ted left her home, Betsie was working in the office when she had a surprise phone call. It was the man from the shipping company and he told her that the ship that Ted was sailing on was coming back to New York, but it would be about another 8 days before the ship would be in the home port. Betsie pondered the news the whole day. Were her prayers answered? Would Ted come home to her? She did not understand her feelings. She tried to calm herself down and not think about all these questions in her mind.

Two days later, she received the last letter from Ted with his request to find some information for him about how to become a United States citizen. She took it upon herself to collect the papers for him and when Ted came back, they would look them over and then make the necessary phone calls.

Chapter 16

The last few days were not that easy for the ship's crew. The weather was cold and miserable. There was a large gale with high waves and the ship's progress was slow, but there was no danger. The skipper, Captain George Baston, was an experienced sailor and Bart had told Ted that he was a very nice person. Bart, Art and the other sailors had sailed with him for two years. They had been through some bad storms in the past but the captain always stayed calm and on course. The first engineer, the second mate and the cook completed the happy sailors' family. They worked most of the day below deck to do some necessary maintenance. They also checked the cargo and tightened everything up.

Only two more days and they would be in the New York harbour. Ted had time to read some more in the little bible. He started to understand more and more of what he was reading and learning, and he applied it to his life. Ted still had to learn how to pray, which was strange to him. Now that they were getting close to home, he realized that when lived at Betsie's home as a family he had enjoyed it, and it made him think about his future and how he might like to have that again.

But all of this is far from reality, he thought. Luckily, the rest of the trip went without any trouble and they arrived safely in the New York harbour. This was the end of Ted's sailing experience but for the rest of the crew, it was just a couple of days at home. The unloading of the cargo went without any trouble and in the afternoon, everybody said goodbye to Ted.

The customs officials came on board and after their inspection was done, Ted would be able to see his Betsie, who had already been waiting for him for over an hour. When they finally saw each other, Ted dropped his bag and took Betsie in his arms and said, "Oh Betsie, I missed you so much!" Betsie had tears in her eyes.

On their drive back home, Ted told her all about what he experienced; the life on board the ship and the friendship with the crew.

Betsie asked him, "Will you go back sailing again?"

He answered, "I will take any job to stay close to you."

Then Ted asked his own question of Betsie, "Betsie, do you want to marry me?"

Betsie answered, "Yes, I do!

That first day at home, the two of them had a lot to talk about. The first thing was that though they were officially in a relationship, they wanted to be married. This was important to Betsie, and she wanted to be married in the church. Ted told her about Bart and what he had taught him about he was reading in the little bible. Ted said that he would like to go with her to the church and begin to live the way she was living.

Betsie was happy to hear all of his plans. She told him that she trusted him and to set a date for their marriage. Ted agreed with her but first, he would need to get a job.

That Sunday, he went with Betsie to the church where he met a few of Betsie's friends. One of them was the man who worked in the harbour office and he told Ted that he would try to get him a job in the harbour. It was difficult because most of the people were union workers. Ted might have to join the union first but the man would try. Another person had a small engineers' office where he could work, but he would start off with a small pay for the first months while he established himself. Ted had to think about all of this. He preferred a job outside and being his own boss, but he would take any job at the moment.

Later at home, Ted and Betsie enjoyed being together and they watched TV. When it was time to go to sleep, he said good night to Betsie and went to his room. He sat on his bed and said a prayer. He thanked the Lord for all his blessings, a prayer he had learned from Bart. As soon as Ted had a reasonable job, Betsie would set a date for their marriage. For the moment, he respected Betsie's wishes.

Chapter 17

The first week back home went by, and the papers for Ted's US citizenship were sent away.

Ted had some appointments for job interviews and with one of them, he had a very good chance for a job he really liked. Two days later, he was contacted to come to the office. He was accepted for a position as maintenance supervisor in the harbour with probation of three months. After that time, if they were satisfied with his work, he would have a full-time job with benefits. He started his job the first day of the new month and when he came home later that night, he felt good and happy. Everything was going well for him and he thanked the Lord every night for his blessings.

He asked Betsie when they were going to set a date to be married, she could not wait to tell him, "As soon as possible!" After they had set a date to get married, they contacted the minister if he was available. With joy in his voice, the minister answered that it would be a pleasure to marry them at that date.

Chapter 18

While Ted was working, he thought about the money he had borrowed from his friend. He did not care about Bolstero as he was a criminal, anyway. He did not want to contact his friend directly because nobody was supposed to know his whereabouts. He did not know what had happened to Bolstero, but he would learn about this later on. Ted told Betsie about his friend and she had an idea. She told Ted that the only way to contact his friend was through another person. Her idea was that the minister of the church could find the address of his friend and then he could contact the friend and send the money for Ted. But first, he had to know the name and if he was the right person. Ted agreed with Betsie so they made an appointment with the minister. This minister would later marry them in their church.

The week started with a surprise phone call from the minister of their church. He said that nobody was looking for Ted anymore and that the man, Bolstero, had passed away. Ted's friend was pleased to hear that he was alive and that he was also pleased and surprised that he was going to pay him back the money he had borrowed from him. For Ted's friend, it came as a miracle because he needed money for his wife. So, it was kind of a coincidence the way everything worked out for all of them. The next day, they gave the minister the money to send to his friend and also a donation to the church.

It did seem that Ted's and Betsie's lives were going in the right direction.

Chapter 19

The wedding between Betsie and Ted was a simple and small occasion with only a reception and a small dinner at the church. The dinner was with some friends from the church and the office where they both were working.

Ted still could not believe what had happened to him. He looked at Betsie when she was talking to their friends and she looked so beautiful and happy. What made him such a lucky fellow who came from the lowest day in his life to rise to this level of happiness? He went to the minister and asked him what he had to do to become a Christian. The minister told him that he was saved when he asked for forgiveness of his sins and accepted the Lord Jesus Christ as his personal Savior. Now, he could be baptised in the church. After that, he should live according to the scriptures and become a member to the church.

Ted felt good about this and he said that he wanted to be baptised as soon as possible. He told the minister about he had read in the bible and that now, he understood the meaning of it. The minister asked him what he had read and Ted answered the way he'd read it in the little bible.

"But search first for the Kingdom of the Lord and his righteousness, and all these things will be added to you".

The minister was surprised with the answer and praised him for his understanding. He told Ted that he would let him know about the baptism the next Sunday they were at the church.

That night, Ted promised Betsie that he would never disappoint her and always would love her. This was the first time they enjoyed each other in love.

Betsie kept working in the soup kitchen and in the harbour office. She sometimes thought of the day she met her new husband and the problems they overcame together. She was so happy and she prayed each night that everything would be forever. Ted was happy with his work and received his full-time position in the harbour. He was baptised and became a member of the church. Bart and Art Bos came to the church to wish him well. Both men would become some of his best friends and stayed in touch with him. He helped Betsie in the soup kitchen and sometimes he helped in the seamens house.

One year later Ted and Betsie were invited to a ceremony for Ted to receive his citizenship and to become an American. It was another step in his new life and now they could travel wherever they wanted.

Chapter 20

It was a summer day and Betsie and Ted were thinking of taking a little vacation. He thought about his parents' possession still in the storage unit in the town where he was living before. Betsie told him that they should go there and to take care of the things in the storage unit to finish dealing with what was left of his past. So, they phoned the bank and made arrangements to close the account, and they went and removed the items in the unit. Most of the things were donated to the local Salvation Army and a few valuable things of precious memories were kept. They visited a few local sceneries before they went back home

They had no problems with the customs when they crossed the border. After a short drive, they stopped by a restaurant for a cup of coffee. When they were having their coffee, a truck driver stepped in the restaurant and Ted could not believe his eyes. He saw that it was Paul and they recognised each other. Ted introduced his wife Betsie to Paul. Paul was so surprised to see Ted and he wanted to know everything about them. Ted could see that Paul was very happy when he told his story and of how he met Betsie.

Paul congratulated him when he heard the news that Ted had found his way to become a Christian. Paul said that he was living in Westchester, a small town not far from New York City, and that he would like Ted and Betsie to come for a visit one day. Ted and Betsie promised to do so.

They exchanged their phone numbers and they promised each other to stay in touch and meet again someday. They were all excited and after their goodbyes, they went on their way home.

Ted felt good that they had closed his past. From now on, they were free of worry. His new life with Betsie and so many good friends that he had met through the last year was just unbelievable.

It had sounded so easy to disappear, or was it the Lord Who pushed him in this direction all along? It was, to Ted, all a miracle.

Epilogue

Sometimes, you are much too occupied with your own way of doing things and do not realize that your life is going in the wrong direction. Sometimes, the Lord will find it necessary to correct the course of your life. Bad things will be changed for the good when you put your eyes on the Lord and believe He is the way.

I believe strongly in this.

Gerry Van Hoorn

Manufactured by Amazon.ca
Bolton, ON